# DIRTY PAKI LINGERIE

By Aizzah Fatima

Foreword by Erica Gould

Afterword by Cobina Gillitt

*NoPassport Press*

*Dirty Paki Lingerie* by Aizzah Fatima

© 2015, 2011 by Aizzah Fatima

All rights reserved. Except for brief passages quoted in newspaper, magazine, radio, or television reviews, no part of this book may be reproduced in any form or by any means, electronic or mechanical, without permission in writing from the author. Professionals and amateurs are hereby warned that this material, being fully protected under the Copyright Laws of the United States of America and of all the other countries of the Berne and Universal Copyright Conventions, is subject to royalty. All rights including, but not limited to professional, amateur, recording, motion picture, recitation, lecturing, public reading, radio and television broadcasting, and the rights of translation into foreign languages are expressly reserved.

Particular emphasis is placed on the question of readings and all uses of this play by educational institutions, permission for which must be secured from the author's representative Sana Hanible, Steinberg Talent Management, 1650 Broadway, Suite 714, NY, NY 10019. Tel: 212-843-3200. Email: stenbergmgr@gmail.com, web: www.steinbergtalent.com

### NoPassport Press

PO Box 1786, South Gate, CA 90280 USA

NoPassportPress@aol.com, www.nopassport.org,

### First Edition.

ISBN: 978-1-312-95918-7

**NoPassport** is a theatre alliance & press devoted to live, virtual and print action, advocacy and change toward the fostering of cross-cultural and aesthetic diversity in the arts.

**NoPassport Press'** Dreaming the Americas Series and Theatre & Performance PlayTexts Series promotes new writing for the stage, texts on theory and practice and theatrical translations.

### Series Editors:

Randy Gener, Jorge Huerta, Mead Hunter, Otis Ramsey-Zoe, Stephen Squibb,

Caridad Svich (founding editor)

### Advisory Board:

Daniel Banks, Amparo Garcia-Crow, Maria M. Delgado, Elana Greenfield, Christina Marin, Antonio Ocampo Guzman, Sarah Cameron Sunde, Saviana Stanescu, Tamara Underiner, Patricia Ybarra

**NoPassport** is a sponsored project of Fractured Atlas. Tax-deductible donations to NoPassport to fund future publications, conferences and performance events may be made directly to
http://www.fracturedatlas.org/donate/2623

# **DIRTY PAKI LINGERIE**

By

Aizzah Fatima

## About the Authors

Playwright:

Aizzah Fatima's solo play *Dirty Paki Lingerie* has been produced in NYC, London, Toronto, Turkmenistan, Pakistan (US State Dept. sponsored four city tour), and The Edinburgh Fringe Festival. She was nominated for an Outstanding Solo Performance award (NYIT 2014). Select acting theatre credits: *Romeo & Juliet* (Access Theatre), Half Hearted (Cherry Lane Theatre), *#serials@theflea* (The Flea Theater), Play by Play Rendezvous (Stageworks Hudson), Circumcaedere (LABrynth Ensemble), *Seven* (Martin E. Segal Theatre Center, Hostos Cultural Arts Center). TV credits: "The Good Wife" (CBS), "Patrice O'Neil's Guide to White People" (Comedy Central), and "Mata-e-jaan" (HUM TV). She has performed at Upright Citizen's Brigade, and in sketches for collegehumor.com. Her short film "Stuff" in which she starred along with Annette O'Toole won the best comedy award (Asians on Film). She is currently working on a feature film based on characters from *Dirty Paki Lingerie* with Emmy award winning director Iman Zawahry.


Foreword:

Erica Gould has directed the world premieres of Neil LaBute's plays *autobahn* and *Stand Up* (with Mos Def) and *SpeakEasy* by Rajiv Joseph, Theresa Rebeck. others (Joe's Pub/Public Theater); the US premieres of *Me Cago en Dios* by Inigo Ramirez de Haro (La MaMa), and *Nobody's Girl* by Rick Viede (NJ Rep); and *Dirty Paki Lingerie*. As director/choreographer: *Max and the Truffle Pig* (NYMF), *City of Angels* (Buffalo), Kander & Ebb's *Curtains*(SDC Guest Artist Initiative); director/fight choreographer:

*Troilus and Cressida* (NY Stage & Film), *The Rover* (Bank Street Theatre), *Pericles* (NJ Shakespeare), *As You Like It* (Shakespeare Theatre ACA), her adaptation of *The Beggar's Opera*; writer/adaptor/director: the music-theatre pieces *More Between Heaven and Earth* (w/ Melissa Errico, Kathleen Chalfant, Campbell Scott, Matthew Modine),*The Heirs of Tantalus*, *Exodus: Dreams of the Promised Land* w/ Reg E Cathey, and *Battalia* (SalonSanctuary/The Fire Dept). Teaching: Yale, NYU, Fordham, Pace, Bard, NYCDA, O'Neill National Theatre Institute. She is the director of *Dirty Paki Lingerie*.

Afterword:

Cobina Gillitt, Ph.D is a freelance dramaturg based in New York City, translator of plays from Indonesian to English, member of Jakarta-based Teater Mandiri, and is currently an Assistant Professor of Theatre and Performance at Purchase College, SUNY. She is the dramaturge for the production of *Dirty Paki Lingerie*.

Aizzah Fatima extends special thanks to Wynn Handman, Matt Hoverman, and Azeez Farooki. NoPassport extends thanks to Catherine Filloux.

Foreword

When Aizzah Fatima first approached me in the early spring of 2011 about working with her on *Dirty Paki Lingerie*, I don't think either of us would have ever imagined the journey that the play has enjoyed. That journey has been an amazing one—from our first production at the Midtown International Theatre Festival in NYC to the show's most recent production in Turkmenistan, from our theatrical runs in Edinburgh and Toronto, to presentations sponsored by educational institutions, the U.S. State Department, and Amnesty International Scotland.

Several months after our first production, we decided to mount a special series of performances of the show in commemoration of the 10th anniversary of the 9/11 attacks. Following each performance, we organized an interfaith panel of scholars, community activists, and religious leaders from the three Abrahamic faiths to discuss their reactions to the play with interested audience members. We were moved and humbled by the impact of many of these discussions, as people from different religious and cultural backgrounds engaged with each other through their emotional and intellectual responses to a work of theatre.

In all of our adventures with the piece, which has evolved over time into the form in which you will read it here, I have been deeply affected by the response to the work from audiences of such wide-ranging cultural, religious, and ethnic backgrounds. When we first started holding post-performance talk-backs, we were not surprised to hear hijabi women in the audience speak about seeing what they felt were their own stories reflected on the stage--something that, as the director of the piece who is Jewish, is always very meaningful to me. But we did not expect an elderly Japanese couple to tell us that they recognized their own story in the experiences of these Muslim-American women, or that a 40-something African-American woman and a 20-something Jewish man would both catch a glimpse of their own lives reflected in the play. *Dirty Paki Lingerie* is a one-woman show that addresses the experience of American-Pakistani women. That something so specific could resonate with people of so many different ethnic, religious, and cultural backgrounds, age ranges, and across gender lines was unexpected to us. That it has done so has confirmed my belief that art may illuminate the universal through an honest exploration of the specific. And I think one of the primary universalities that the piece taps into is that of the American "hyphenated" experience, the commonality of the immigrant journey, whether one's family has been here for five months or five generations. There is an inherent tension between what has been left behind and what we take with us, between the impulse to assimilate, and the desire to maintain our identity, between what we hold onto and what we fear we may have forgotten. All of the characters in the play struggle with some iteration of this dilemma, and the Prologue and the Epilogue, which form the frame for the play and which are quite different stylistically from everything that falls between them, speak to this issue eloquently and directly with poetic text both new and centuries old, forming the prism through which the rest of the piece may be understood. As the play begins, a disembodied voice is heard, and then a woman's face, at first only barely perceptible, begins to emerge behind a great sheath of silk, illuminated by the projection of fragments of Urdu text--the words of the poet Mirza Ghalib, written hundreds of years ago, yet speaking so directly to the dreams and longings and heartbreak of the contemporary characters who populate the play. As the Urdu text transforms into its English translation, this woman, a poet herself, struggles to remember a forgotten verse, and the words disintegrate around her, breaking apart and cascading to the floor. Perhaps they cannot be remembered in English. Perhaps they belong to a different world, a different culture, a different century. Perhaps she has not yet experienced enough in her life for them to come back to her. The veil that all the characters will use in different ways is separated from the huge swath of green silk and the Poet heads off on her journey, leaving the rest of her history behind. We follow the stories of Ameera, the recent immigrant; Selma, the all-American hijabi feminist; 6-year-old Zahra; 65-year-old Asma; Hiba; Raheela... And at the end of the journey we have taken with these characters, we meet the Poet again, writing stories about the possibilities for a young woman's journey, about the choices we make, about what we sacrifice and leave behind, about what we wish for. And then she remembers that forgotten Urdu verse and we see it emerge from within the folds of the fabric she had discarded. As if it had been there all along but she could not see it. And yet it disintegrates in the moment of remembering, like an ancient fragment of parchment, or fabric, preserved and forgotten for centuries, that disintegrates the moment it is exposed to the air, or like a dream that disappears from our consciousness the moment we try to describe it. And it is still not enough. We must straddle the worlds of our past and present to create our future and that is an uneasy and tenuous balance, like words delicately hovering, fragile, in the folds of an expanse of green silk. DPL is filled with funny, insightful, and emotionally moving text and characters that, after all this time, I find I do not tire of, and continue to enjoy staging and re-staging in the various venues and countries in which we have found ourselves so fortunate to be asked to present the play. But I think that the extraordinary, haunting text Aizzah created that we have used for the Prologue and Epilogue is what moves me most deeply, and has most inspired me as a director in finding a theatrical, physical, visual language to tell this story.

That the play ends with a question has always seemed fitting to me; that it is a question to the audience, more fitting still. And it is a play that begins and ends with the words of poets --Mirza Ghalib and Aizzah Fatima.

I often tell my students that theatre is about giving away--the playwright gives the play to the director, the director gives the play to the actor, and the actor gives the play to the audience for whom it was created. With this publication, we now give it to you, the reader, joyously sending the play off into the world in a different way, to speak on its own without us.

Erica Gould

# DIRTY PAKI LINGERIE

A Solo Play

by Aizzah Fatima

## Cast of Characters

POET: A young dreamer

AMEERA: 20 years old, a visitor to America

SELMA: 22 years old, an American-Pakistani hijabi feminist

ZARA: 6 years old, a school girl

MRS SHAH: 65 years old, an American-Pakistani mother

RAHEELA: 35 years old, an American-Pakistani business woman

HIBA: 55 years old, a teacher, wife, and mother

### Place
In and around New York City.

### Time
Present day.

## PROLOGUE

SETTING: A rectangular black wooden box is placed center stage with an opening in the back for storing props. There is a window upstage left with a green fabric hanging over it. The Fabric extends diagonally onto the stage.

> POET V.O.
> (In the dark, we hear a disembodied voice.)

In the 18th century, the great urdu poet Mirza Ghalib wrote: "Hazaroon khwahishain Aisi ke her khwahish pe dum nikle"

> (The verse of the poem is projected on the green fabric written in Urdu. An isolated face becomes discernible behind the green fabric.)

I have a thousand wishes that I would die for. I have always loved that poem... but I cannot remember... the second... verse.

> (The Urdu poetry disintegrates and descends as light gradually expands to reveal the POET. She is dressed in all black. As we hear her thoughts, she moves simply about the stage extending the green fabric. The lighting is dream-like, hallucinatory.)

I am writing a story about a girl who grows up in a small town always dreaming of moving to the big city. She does not like her small town. She imagines the big city will be a beautiful place. It will be clean, and full of happy clean people instead of the dirty people in her small town. She will live in a huge house with big glass windows. Every day she will visit beautiful gardens full of roses, gardenias, and jasmine. In the big city, the sun will shine through her window to wake her up. Not like in her small town which is hidden between two mountains, and never sees the sun. And one day her dream comes true and it is everything she ever imagined and much more.

> (The POET rips a small piece from the large green fabric and takes it with her. Leaving the rest of it behind. She wraps the green fabric around herself while continuing the movement.)

I have a thousand wishes that I would die for…Hazaroon Khwahishain Aisi ke her khwahish pe dum nikle.

## Scene 1:

>(Suddenly the lights are very bright, and Justin Timberlake's "Sexy Back" is blasting. AMEERA, a 20 year old Pakistani girl, is trying out dance moves. She rubs the dupata on her body attempting to be sexy. She speaks with a Pakistani accent, and bounces around never sitting in one place for too long. There is something innocent, child like about her. She is in her cousin's apartment in NYC.)

>            AMEERA
>(She hears her cousin, Annie, and stops dancing.)

What? What, Annie? The music is too loud?

>(Lowers volume.)

Why do you look like someone beat you with a shoe? Really? You want to listen to Mirza Ghalib right now? Okay.

>(Turns off Justin Timberlake. Puts on Mirza Ghalib.)

You should listen to Britney Spears and Justin Timberlake. Now that is great poetry.

>(Singing and dancing)

I'm bringing sexy back. Yeah. Them other boys don't know how to act. Yeah.
Ghalib is an old fart.

(Turns off music)

And he's dead. His music is depressing. Do you need Prozac? I saw on tv if you are depressed you can take this pill Prozac, and it works like magic.

(Bored)

I know, I know... "Hazaroon khwahishain Aisi ke her khwahish pe dum nikle"

(Then more excited)

I have a thousand wishes that are all going to come true in America! Annie, I still can't believe I'm here in New York City with you my lovely cousin. And your mom and dad are so generous for letting me stay here while I find a nice Pakistani American doctor to marry. Annie, is it true? You can have all your dreams come true in America. I saw it in Eddie Murphy movie - Coming to America. He is quite handsome.

(Whisper as if sharing a secret)

Even though he is black.

(She jumps up and starts folding the green fabric.)

Why do you listen to Ghalib's depressing poetry? You live in a beautiful home and your parents let you go to college three hours away! And there is always hot water and the electricity never goes out.

When I tell people we had servants in Pakistan, they think we must be very rich. They don't realize every middle class family in Pakistan has someone to clean for them. Even the servants have servants. You can always find someone more poor than you.

I don't know why some Pakistanis back home hate America so much. I saw a beggar on the train yesterday with a $20 bill in a plastic bottle. That is 2000 rupees. If beggars back home had that much money they could eat for two weeks. And he had a sign that said, "Will work for food." Even beggars here have a good work ethic.

## Scene 2:

(The stage quickly grows dark, and we hear the Call to Prayer. The light isolates the actor, who extends the scarf, and slowly turns as she drapes it about her. The effect is beautiful and dream like. When she turns to face the audience again, she is in a full hijab – Islamic head covering. She is SELMA, a 22 year old woman. She speaks with an American accent. She kneels and prays.)

SELMA
(She turns head to right shoulder.)
Asalaamu Alikum Wa Rehmat Allah.
(She turns head to left shoulder.)
Asalaamu Alikum Wa Rehmat Allah
(Sound of loud knocking on the door.)
Ameer, what do you want. Dork.
(Knocking continues)
Stop knocking! I'm busy?
(She covers her face with her hands.)
Asalaamu Alikum Wa Rehmat Allah.
(Raises hands together to pray.)
God please help me get a 30 or above on the MCAT exam so I can get into medical school. If I get a 30 or above, then I promise to fast for 10 days.
(Beat)

Okay, I'll fast for 5 days.

> (Beat)

Okay, I will honestly do it for 3 days. I know I owe you 10 days from last semester but I promise to really do it this time.

> (Loud knocking again.)

Ameer! What? Oh. Well, why didn't you tell her to come in? Dork.

> (Raises hands together to pray again.)

Sorry – okay, I promise to do it for 13 days.

> (All in one breath.)

God, please help me stay away from all the sins of the world, and guide me on the right path. Ameen.

> (Greets Sadia excitedly at the door.)

OMG! Sadia, get in here. What took you so long? Close the door.

> (Takes out a white envelope.)

Here it is!, I can't open it. You do it.

> (Hands it to Sadia, but snatches it back before Sadia can open it.)

No! Wait! Let's sit and talk for a minute. Then we'll open it. I haven't even told my parents I got it yet.

> (SELMA places the envelope on the black box.)

No, I don't want to go to some stupid Caribbean school. Aww, you are so sweet. You really think I could get into Harvard? I would need a really high score for that, but how awesome would that be if I could actually go to Harvard. I wish! I would need to get at least a 30 to get in. They have the best pediatric program.

>               (beat)
>
> Augh, ok I don't want to talk about it any more. I went shopping today. Let me show you what I got.
>
>               (She goes to one of the green bags
>               placed up stage. Takes out a racy
>               piece of red lingerie, and holds it up
>               close to her body)
>
> This is for the wedding night. No, I didn't try it on. I went shopping with my Mom. The only person who will ever see me in this is Shahid.
>
>               (She places the lingerie back in the
>               bag.)
>
> Well, if I can't wear that for my future husband than who can I wear it for? Sadia, you sound like one of my Mom's friends from Pakiland, criticizing Arab Muslim women for wearing revealing clothing in the privacy of their own home. At least they aren't doing it for the whole world to see, like a piece of meat for every man to ogle. Like this woman on the subway the other day, wearing, like, nothing. OMG! She was like.

                 WOMAN ON SUBWAY
What the fuck is you lookin' at? FUCK you, ASSHOLE. Lookin' at me like I ain't got no clothes on? FUCK you.

                      SELMA
                 (Looks up at ceiling.)
Sorry God.

At least I respect myself enough to not let men objectify me. I feel more liberated covering myself up than the

women who walk down the street half naked. It really bothers me and Shahid that people associate the hijab with oppression. Talk about oppression. We couldn't even pass the equal rights amendment here. (This text may be substituted for another current event)
We don't need European feminists to celebrate topless jihad day. We just need to have the right to choose.
OMG! You have to swear, swear, swear not to ever tell anyone I said this.

(Beat)

In High school I thought feminists were lesbians who hate men.

(Beat)

If women here really had the right to choose, then that Congress woman in Michigan wouldn't have gotten thrown out of the state house for saying the word vagina. The Republicans are like the Taliban. And the Taliban don't practice true Islam. Islam gave women the right to own property while women in Europe were still being treated like cattle.
You know, Sadia, when I first started covering my hair, my parents thought I would never get married. They didn't think any guys here would like me if I covered my hair. My dad was like:

DAD

Beta ji it is not safe to cover your hair with all that is going on. You know after 9/11 it is not safe for us to do these things openly.

SELMA

It's not like we live in France, Dad. And my parents' friends are like:

### PARENT'S FRIEND

Oh! She covers her hair. And she is friends with the black people. What good family will want her to marry their son?

### SELMA

And then they complain it's racist here. And how the food is too bland, and how every time a bomb goes off any where they blame America.
(Beat)
If they hate it here so much, why don't they go back to their own country. Because it sucks there. That's why. Sadia, it does. Salman Taseer was killed in Pakistan by his own security guard for standing up against corrupt blasphemy laws.
I know things are not perfect here either. Some guy with a US passport and no criminal record gets thrown in jail because his name is Mohammed. That's like John.
Shahid and his parents get all this stuff. Unlike my parents and their friends. When I talk to them about this, all they have to say is che che che Bechara. I'm telling Shehnaz Auntie about all this the other day, and she says.

### SHEHNAZ AUNTIE

I don't know anything about such things, but what I do know is, you should keep it clean down there. Just wax all the hairs. Your husband will like it.

### SELMA

Ewww. TMI. TMI.

>(Sees envelope)

Should I open it? What if I got lower than a 30. Oh, God. I can't open it now.

>(Holds up another piece of lingerie.)

Okay, what do you think about this one? Seriously? You think Shahid will like it?

>(Puts it back and takes out another piece of lingerie. Each piece gets progressively more racy.)

Okay, well, what about this one? What. Would you rather I wear this?

>(Holds up flannel grannie nightgown. Beat.)

Sadia, what is it? You can tell me. You are like my sister.

>(Beat)

What? I can't believe Shahid asked you not to come to the wedding. Why would he do that. Unless… a couple of days ago we were talking, and I told him I had kissed some guys before I started covering my hair, and he wanted to know which of my friends knew about my past, and I told him the only one I share everything with is you.

>(Beat)

You are coming to my wedding. You're like my sister. There's no one else in the world I would want to be my maid of honor. I'm going to talk to him about this. This is all going to get sorted out.

>(Looks at envelope)

I'm going to open this now.

>(Takes the envelope out, and opens it. Reads it, shocked.)

It's a 38. I got a 38. I can't believe it. I can probably get into Harvard with a 38 --

> (Stops abruptly)

But Shahid is starting Law School here in the fall.

> (Beat)

How can I marry Shahid, and go to Harvard. Of course he would want what's best for me. But no, I can't ask him to do that. Although, he...would do that for me...

> (The lights darken around her, trapping her.)

I know he would.

> (She is isolated in a narrow box of light.)

I know he would.

## Scene 3:

(SELMA turns upstage as we hear Mirza Ghalib music. The scarf drops to her shoulders to reveal AMEERA. She talks to Annie in her bedroom.)

### AMEERA

Annie, even I feel like listening to Ghalib today. With my good looks, I thought it would be easy to find a nice-Pakistani-American-doctor to marry.

(She turns off the music.)

My visa is only for six months, and every guy I meet is worse than the last. I thought guys here would be different and better than in Pakistan. But not so far. The last few guys I met were the worst.

### GUY 1

(Stern)

We'll BOTH have the steak. Let me butter that ROLL for you.

### GUY 2

(Lights a cigarette and blows smoke at AMEERA.)

My dad owns three laundromats. I don't see the point in working.

(Scratches his armpit and smells his fingers.)

When he dies all of his money will go to me any way. Why do I need to work?

25

## GUY 3
You are not really my type. I like blonde girls. My parents are making me meet paki girls. If it works out between us, do you think you could die your hair? Down there?


## AMEERA
And then there are the guys on Muslimmatrimony.com. Half of them are balding, and they put up this picture from when they were 18 I think, and now they are 30. I am almost 21 years old. Next year who will want to marry me? There is this other guy, Rayaan. He friended me on Facebook? He wants to marry me, but he lives in California. He is not so good looking. But Ammi always says for a guy it's not important to look good. He has a good job. And I sent him this one picture where these bug bites
                    (Grabs her breasts)
look like big juicy mangoes. Now he thinks I'm hot. But I'm not so sure.

## Scene 4:

>(We hear the theme song from Dora the Explorer. The scarf slips around her waist, and she bounces along to the music. It is ZARA. She is 6 years old.)

>ZARA
>(Talks to herself while pointing in the book.)

She's a princess and she's a princess and she's a princess. This is me, this is Laila, and this is Mom.

>(Dora music turns off.)

Mommy, Laila turned off Dora.

>(Looks in book.)

I'm gonna choose pink.

>(ZARA reaches behind her, and takes out a 2 inch Dora dall. She plays with the doll throught the scene. Talks to the doll in secrecy.)

I like pink because pink is my favorite color. And these have pink sparkles. Hey here's pink. She's smiling. I want…

>(To her 3 year old sister Laila who tries to take away her Dora doll.)

Swiper no swiping…Swiper no swiping…Laila no swiping….Laila no swiping.

>(Wags her finger in Laila's face.)

Laila, you are inappropriate.

>(To her Mom upstage.)

27

No, I don't want goldfish right now. I don't want to eat cheese. I like cheese, but I'm not gonna eat cheese right now. Mommy can I have ice cream?

(Beat)

Mommy, tomorrow can you pack me a sandwich like Emma K's Mom. I don't want roti for lunch. I like roti at home, but I don't like it at school.

Laila, no swiping. Mommy, no, I don't want to share Dora. Laila always cries to get her way. She's stu--

Nah ah - I wasn't gonna say stupid Mom. I was just gonna say stu. She gets everything because she's the baby. It's not fair. Can we get the big Dora doll like Daddy promised?

(Beat)

When can we get it Mom? Daddy said I could get it for my birthday. I haven't seen daddy in

(Counts on fingers.)

Uno, dos, tres, one, two, three…three months. Uncle Waseem said the policeman took daddy because he has the same name as a bad guy. A bad guy who goes to jail. Sameer at the Sunday school class at the mosque said that a police man was spying on our class Mommy, and he was also spying on the halal chicken restaurant. Maybe daddy is helping the spy policeman.

(Beat)

Mom, this boy at school Joe Johnson he kissed me, and it was inappropriate. I told him he's a stinky stupid stu. And he called me a terra-mist and he said…he said…he said.

## JOE JOHNSON

Go back to your own country. You Osama lover terra-mist.

## ZARA

I said you are a terra-mist, and I kicked my foot, and he put his face in front of it. So he got a kick in his face. That was funny.

Member when I was playing foot sweep with daddy, and he got my foot in his face. That was funny too.

Mommy I don't wanna play foot sweep with you. I wanna play it with daddy. It's a daddy game.

Laila no swiping. Mom, I don't want to share my Dora doll with anyone. It's mine. She can have the Diego doll. I…

> (ZARA gets up and confronts her mom.)

No, Mom I don't wanna share it. Mommy, you are inappropriate. I'm gonna put you in jail. I won't give it to Laila. She's just a baby and she ruins all my toys. No I won't give it. I hate Laila. I hate you. I hate you. Laila is stupid, and you are stupid.

> (Her mother starts to cry. ZARA is shocked, and stares at her Mom for a few beats not knowing what to do. ZARA crouches down lower and lower on the floor as her Mom hits the floor crying.)

Mom. Mommy. Mom, don't cry. You want Dora?

> (Extends Dora to Mom)

You can have Dora Mom.

## Scene 5:

>(ZARA swirls around, and the scarf goes on her head as we see ASMA. ASMA hums an old Indian song "Tum agar saath daine ka wada kero main yoon hi mast naghme luta ta rahoon." She shakes her head from side to side. She walks over to the box and first takes out a newspaper, then a phone with a cord, and finally a pen.)

>ASMA
>(Looks in newspaper and dials a number.)

Hello, Asalaamu Alikum. My name is Mrs. Shah I am calling from New Jersey about your ad in the Urdu Times Matrimonial section. I see you live in Chicago. The boy live in Chicago also? Oh, he live in Pakistan. Acha.

>(Disappointed she shakes her head and places a big X in the newspaper.)

No, I am looking in the US only. You know it is hard to adjust for people coming from Pakistan. My daughter come to this country when she is 20 year old, but she like boys born and raised in the US only. Okay, I have friend looking for nice boy in Pakistan. I will give her your number. Khuda hafiz.

>(Looks in newspaper and dials another number.)

Hello, Asalaamu Alikum. My name is Mrs. Shah I am

calling from New Jersey about your ad in the Urdu Times Matrimonial section.

Yes, yes, I know he is doctor. How much is the boy making? Ok very good. Mashallah.

Skin color? She is you know not too dark. Wheat-ish. Oh, he want fair skinned girl. You know these days with make up everyone can look fair skinned. She is very beautiful girl, you know? I say let the children talk on the email, the tweetering, the bookface, and then they decide. You know we are all Pakistani. Our girls don't look like the white girls with the beelond hairs.

>(Beat)

Okay. Khuda Hafiz.

>(She hangs up the phone.)

## Scene 6:

> (We hear the sounds of a noisy airport terminal. ASMA slips the scarf from her head and ties it around her neck to reveal RAHEELA. RAHEELA is a 35 year old American-Pakistani woman. She is stylish and professional. She stands, gathers her bags, and places a wireless piece in her ear. She is speaking to a friend.)

### RAHEELA

Hey. I'm at the airport. My flight's delayed. It took forever to get through security. I just want to sit down. Oh great. It's packed. And this fat desi auntie wearing her shalwaar kameez, and eating her paratha out of a paper bag is taking up two seats with all her crap.

> (RAHEELA walks up to PARATHA LADY)

Excuse me. Can I sit here?

> (PARATHA LADY doesn't respond as if she can't speak English.
> RAHEELA rolls her eyes annoyed.)

Main idher baith sakti hoon.

> (Beat)

Thank you.

> (Raheela speaks to her friend on the phone.)

Gotta love that desi smell. Chillax, she doesn't understand English.

(She takes her cell phone out of her
bag, and spots a cute guy sitting
across from her as she places her bag
on the floor.)

Oh my God, this super cute guy is sitting across from me.
No. On the other side. Oh my God, he just looked at me.

(She looks back at the guy. He's still
looking at her.)

He's like totally checking me out. I am not making this up.
He really is. If Brad Pitt and Matt Damon had a brown love
child, he would look like this guy. Oh my God, he just
waved at me.

(She waves back.)

He's really hot. You're not going to believe this. He just
wrote his number on a newspaper and is holding it up for
me. I'm going to take down his number. Do you think I
should text him? I'm gonna text him.

(RAHEELA reads the text outloud
as she types.)

Hi it's Raheela. Send.

(Into the phone.)

Augh that was stupid.

(sound of incoming text)

Oh wait. He wrote back.

(RAHEELA reads his response.)

I'm Hassan, and I don't usually do this sort of thing.

(RAHEELA talks into the phone.)

Oh my God. What should I say? Oh, I know. Okay.

(RAHEELA types)

I do this sort of thing all the time. LOL. Smiley face. Send.
Oh my God. I can't believe I just said that.

(Beat)

He's not writing back. Shit! Do you think it was too forward? Fuck. I fucked it up. Fuck.

(Sound of incoming text.)

Oh wait. He wrote back.

(RAHEELA reads the text)

You are so beautiful.

(Into the phone.)

Oh my God! He thinks I'm beautiful. Okay, what should I say?

(Sound of incoming text.)

Oh wait. He just sent something else.

(Into the phone.)

He's asking me if I live in Chicago. How should I answer that? Oh. Right. I just tell him.

(Types)

No. Send.

(Into the Phone.)

Oh God! That sounds unfriendly. Smiley face. Send.

(Sound of incoming text.)

He's asking me where I live.

(Types)

Manhattan. Upper East Side

(PARATHA LADY does something annoying. RAHEELA looks over at her. Sound of incoming text.)

Can you believe this? He lives ten blocks from me.

(RAHEELA types)

Maybe we could get together for dinner sometime.

(She gasps and then proceeds to delete the message.)

Delete. Delete. Delete. Delete. Delete.
                        (Thinks for moment then types.)
Do you like your apartment?
                        (She hits send then is mortified.)
 Augh!!!

## Scene 7:

>(The sound of the airport morphs into the sounds of a crowded restaurant.
>RAHEELA's scarf slips around her shoulders and she is AMEERA.
>AMEERA runs to a corner of the stage. She crouches in the corner. She is in a cramped restaurant bathroom.
>She dials her cell phone.)

AMEERA

Come on, Annie, pick up! Pick up! I have to talk to you.
>(It goes to voicemail.)

Annie, it's me. Why aren't you here at the restaurant? Rayaan, the guy from Facebook, is already here. And his family. And your mom and dad. We had the appetizer already. I'm calling you from the bathroom.

He is not so cute. Now I'm not so sure. His brother is much cuter. I don't really love him. Ammi always says don't marry the one you love. Marry the one who loves you because he will take care of you his whole life. Why aren't you here? Should I do it? I mean he got a ring and everything. He flew all the way out here from California with his sister, his parents, and his brother. You know the cute one. Maybe I should just do it. I haven't really met anyone else here, and my visa is running out soon. Where are you Annie? They probably have served dinner by now. Okay, I have to go someone is knocking on the bathroom

door.
>(Beat)

I guess I'll marry him.
>(Ameera stares at the phone. Then turns it off.)

### Scene 8:

>(Lights shift to bright. AMEERA turns, bringing the scarf over her head, humming the same song from before "Tum agar saath daine ka wada kero main yoon hi mast naghme luta ta rahoon." We see ASMA who takes out her pen, newspaper, and the phone with a cord.
>She settles in then looks in newspaper and dials a number.)

#### ASMA

Hello, Asalaamu Alikum. My name is Mrs. Shah I am calling from New Jersey about your ad in the Urdu Times Matrimonial section?
What does boy do? Oh, computer engineer. Very nice. Very nice. How old is boy?

>(Writes on newspaper.)

Okay forty-two or forty-three. Okay. Yes, My daughter is about thirty-two, thirty four. Oh, you are looking for someone a little younger?

>(Beat)

But she look very young. Like still in high school. You know kids these days like to exercise, and she eat very little like bird. I understand. Okay. Khuda Hafiz.

>(Looks in newspaper, and dials another number.)

Hello, Asalaamu Alikum. My name is Mrs. Shah. I am calling from New Jersey about your ad in the Urdu Times matrimonial section. Yes, how are you doing? I have one daughter. She is about thir-- Twenty-seven, twenty-nine. And light skinned. How old is boy? He is thirty-five.

                (Mutters to herself)

Very good.

                (Into the phone.)

What does boy do? Very nice he drive cab. My daughter is architect. You know. They make big building. Yes, oh no, she is expert cook. I teach her myself. She even cook better than me. Not like girl born and brought up here.

But you know these days all girls work and they cook and clean. Maybe after they have children, then she stay at home. You know? Oh, too educated. No, no I understand. Okay Khuda Hafiz.

## Scene 9:

>(ASMA slams the phone. Lights shift and ASMA drops the scarf from her head to her shoulders. She turns into HIBA. HIBA puts on her sunglasses, and picks up her bag. She looks around the room as if looking for someone. She seats herself at a table and looks at a menu. She looks up and spots someone coming toward her. She waves and motions for the person to sit.)

>                HIBA

I feel so old with all these hip college kids around. The menu looks great though. I'm glad we have a few moments alone.

>                (Beat)

You know I was only seventeen when I married your father. It was the summer after I graduated from high school. While my former classmates were heading off to college, I was heading off to Pakistan from Queens for my marriage ceremony.

I never told you this before, but I was all set to marry someone else two days before I married your father. I didn't know him. Amma and Aba ji picked him out for me. Then two days before the wedding Abba ji found out that Ilyaas, that was his name, was doing drugs.

Abba Ji was all about appearances. He couldn't be disgraced in the community by bringing his daughter back to Queens without her being married. So he found me a substitute.

(Beat)

Your father.

### Scene 10:

>(Lights shift again and we are inside. HIBA places the scarf on her head and turns into ASMA. She picks up the phone.)

### ASMA
Hello Asalaamu Alikum. My name is Mrs. Shah. I am calling from New Jersey about your ad in the Urdu Times matrimonial section.
>(She is cut off abruptly.)

She is you know good height for Pakistani girl...over 5 feet. About...5'1" or so. Hello? Hello?

### Scene 11:

(ASMA turns quickly. The phone is gone, and AMEERA is talking to Annie in Annie's room. AMEERA frantically walks in circles.)

### AMEERA

Annie! I had to come see you! I have to tell you something. No, I'm not okay. Rayaan…uff..I can't tell you. Last night after the wedding we went to the hotel room. He took off all of his clothes and…I can't tell you…his banana….he doesn't even have a banana. It just hangs there like the root of a hundred year old tree. Have you ever seen such a thing in a young man? He can't get it up. And he said are you going to leave me if I can't get it up. Don't you love me. He says he's never had this problem before. His is very small …maybe just 2 inches…and it just sits there. I looked at pictures on Google and saw some videos on you tube Annie. I know what it should look like. It's just very small.

### Scene 12:

>(AMEERA turns quickly to reveal ASMA. The phone is back in her hand, and the scarf is back on her head.)

>              ASMA

Hello. Asalaamu Alikum, My name is Mrs. Shah. I am calling from...
What does the boy do? What kind of business. And he own the gas station? His uncle own the gas station. That's nice!

>(Looks down at paper.)

Yes, I see he divorced once. He is having children also? How many? They live with the mother of course. No? They live with you? Does he live with you?
That's nice. I will call later tonight to get your details. Oh no, no, no don't call me. I will call you. Okay? Khuda Hafiz.

>(ASMA slams the phone.)

## Scene 13:

(ASMA Turns and we see RAHEELA, scarf around her neck. Lights are suddenly dark all around her, and we hear the low hum of an airplane engine. The quiet of an airplane when most people are asleep.

RAHEELA is enjoying a glass of wine while IM'ing on her laptop. Her IMs are projected behind her.)

PROJECTION: I know what you are saying, but I also think that those kinds of images can be part of the problem.

(Sound of incoming IM.)

RAHEELA

Okay sure. It was also about the relationships and racial tensions in that community. But...

PROJECTION: Everyone is a stereotype. The black people don't have jobs. The Asian people can't speak any English. And the white people are, of course, racist.

(Sound of incoming IM. RAHEELA reads, laughs, then to herself.)

RAHEELA

No. It wasn't the Cosby Show.

PROJECTION: I do think Do The Right Thing is a good

film, but Malcolm X's quote at the end? Calling violence a form of intelligence, really?

>(Sound of incoming IM.)

RAHEELA

You know

PROJECTION: From the people's perspective the Arab Spring was non-violent. It's those governments that are violent.

>(Sound of outgoing IM. Then to herself.)

RAHEELA

I can't fucking see anything with this glare.
>(RAHEELA turns to PARATHA LADY.)

Excuse me Aunty. There's a glare coming in from the window. Can you pull the shade?
>(The woman doesn't understand English. RAHEELA grunts in frustration.)

Augh!!
>(Then to PARATHA LADY)

Window se glare aa rahi hai. Is ko thora neechay kerain gay? What were the chances of me getting stuck next to her?

>(Sound of incoming IM.)

My favorite book?

PROJECTION: Definitely, To Kill a Mockingbird.

(Sound of incoming IM.)
You own three copies of it?

PROJECTION: Me too! I have to buy a copy anytime I see one at a used book store.
(Sound of incoming IM.)

RAHEELA

Aww. I love the idea of naming a daughter Harper.

PROJECTION: Much better than naming her Boo. My favorite part is at the end when Scout recaps everything.
(Sound of incoming IM. Beat.)

RAHEELA

Oh my God. I can't believe you know that by heart.
(Sound of incoming IM. RAHEELA reads, and then types.)

PROJECTION: I would love to do this in person. Maybe we can get together for coffee when we're both back in the city.
(Sound of incoming IM.)

RAHEELA

Sooner?

PROJECTION: Sure. I don't know what my schedule is going to be in Chicago, but
(Sound of incoming IM.)

RAHEELA

Why don't you meet me now...in the... first class...bathroom.

(Beat. Then types.)

PROJECTION: Okay.

(RAHEELA slowly closes her laptop and puts it away. The PARATHA LADY wants to go to the aisle, RAHEELA makes room for her, then hears her say something under her breath. RAHEELA gets up and follows PARATHA LADY into the aisle.)

RAHEELA

Excuse me? So you understand English now?
First of all it's none of your business lady. And second, why am I a slutty girl? What about him? Why aren't you calling him a slutty guy? What about all those men in your beloved country who have two wives?
This is what guys like him do, right? They want to talk to someone like me, spend time with someone like me, and sleep with someone like me, but they'll never marry someone like me. They all want to marry a virgin. A virgin who is twenty-two. I know he won't marry me. And I don't care about marrying him. Life is too short lady. Why don't you live a little, and mind your own business you fat

fucking cow!

>(RAHEELA walks down the airplane aisle back towards her seat. She hesitates for a long moment. Then walks defiantly and sadly towards the first-class bathroom.)

## Scene 14:

>(The lights change, ASMA places scarf on her head and turns. The sound of the plane is gone, and ASMA has a phone with a cord in her hand, but no newspaper. She dials a phone number.)

>### ASMA

Hello Bilal. Betay, this is your mother calling. Pick up phone. Are you there? Hello? Hello?
Hello, Bilal? Don't you have any good Muslims friend for your sister? You know it is your Islamic duty as older brother to get her married. Okay?
You know it is her birthday today, and she is already thirty-two thirty-four. What am I to do? My only daughter thirty-two, thirty-four not getting married.
Dramatic? Don't tell me I'm being dramatic. I am not doing drama shrama for your entertainment okay? She come over yesterday, she say she... I'm worried she might...

>(Beat)

Just round up your good Muslim friends, Okay? And bring them over for my Eid party next week. Okay?
Okay. Khuda Haf...Hey wait! What about you? I send you ten pretty girl picture. You don't like? Are you the gay? Okay. No, no. I am just saying. I am your mother! Okay beta. You take your time. Khuda Hafiz.

>(Lets out a big sigh a little depressed.
>Sinks into chair, dials another number on phone.)

Hello Najma, this is Asma calling from New Jersey. Can you find out if that doctor boy in Pakistan is still available for my Sidra. You know the one that want 25 year old girl only. Yes, just send them the old picture of her I gave you five year ago. Okay. Khuda Hafiz.

                        (ASMA hangs up the phone.)

## Scene 15:

>(The lights grow bright, and we hear the sound of birds. We are outside. HIBA drapes her scarf around her shoulders, and holds the menu in her lap.)

### HIBA

Your father was happy to substitute for the groom two days before the wedding. Who didn't want to come to the U.S. in those days? Marrying me was a free ticket to the U.S. for your father's entire family. I felt like the luckiest girl when I saw your father. Your father was tall, and handsome. I will never forget what Amma said to me that day.

### AMMA

He is out of your league. He is handsome and educated. You are lucky his family is poor, and they have agreed to marry him to you. Hold onto him. Be obedient, and learn to cater to his every wish.

### HIBA

And I believed her.
No one ever asked me what I wanted. I wanted to go to law school, but your father didn't like that. He needed me to be home to take care of you and your brother, and to cook three meals a day. So I left law school in the middle of my first year. I was a dutiful daughter, and an obedient wife. Just like I was taught to be. Any time I had doubts about my new married life with your father, Amma's voice

echoed in my mind.

### AMMA

We are not like the Amreekans. You have to remember your culture, and where you come from. We are Pakistani. You grow where you are planted.

### HIBA
(To herself)

You grow where you are planted.
(Beat)

Honey, I am so proud of you for getting into law school and graduating with honors. I'm very proud. I love you, and your brother. If there is one accomplishment I'm proud of in my life, it's the two of you.
(Beat)

I asked your father to move out of the house.
(Beat)

Yesterday.

I'm fifty-five years old, and I want to live the rest of my life on my terms not your fathers. I don't want to live in fear of what my family will say or his family or the people in the community.

I wanted to leave 20 years ago, but my Mom convinced me to stay.

## AMMA

This is nonsense. Respectful Muslim daughters don't leave their husband. We are not like the Amreekans. There is no divorce in our culture. You leave your husband's house when you die. That's it.

## HIBA

I'm tired of living with a man who doesn't love me. I'm tired of worrying about what respectful Muslim daughters should and shouldn't do. I don't want to be sixty years old, and look back at my life with regrets. No one should have to do that.

(Beat)

I want you to know I've met someone. Ahmed teaches with me at the school. We've been friends for years.

(Beat)

He's wonderful. He asks me what I want.

(Beat)

Your father knows.

(Beat)

Promise me that you will never compromise your hopes and dreams for a man. Don't ever marry a man out of obligation. Marry a man because you love him. Just promise me that.

**EPILOGUE**

>              (We hear a disembodied voice.)

>              POET V.O.

There was a young girl who was a poet.

>              (HIBA gets up, picks up her things,
>              and gets ready to leave the cafe.)

She lived in a small town, but dreamed of living in the big city.
One day she met a magical fairy who agreed to grant her one wish.

>              (HIBA leaves the cafe and puts
>              down her bag, facing upstage.)

She wished that she could live in the big city in a huge house with big glass windows.
The fairy granted her wish, but told the girl she would never remember her small town.

>              (HIBA looks back, over her
>              shoulder, towards the stage.)

And never remember the way back home. The girl agreed.

>              (As the lights start to darken HIBA
>              turns and becomes the POET. Lights
>              gradually change to dream like,
>              hullucinatory. The Poet continues
>              her story moving slowly and
>              deliberately through the space,
>              putting away RAHEELA's laptop,
>              ASMA's newspaper, and SELMA's
>              envelope, etc.)

In the big city, she lived in a huge house with big glass windows. A city with beautiful gardens full of roses,

gardinias, and jasmine. A city that was clean and full of happy clean people. One day she looked out the big glass windows and tried to write a poem.
     (POET stops)
But could not remember how. She could not remember her small town. She could not remember the way back home.
     (POET resumes moving through the
     space gathering things.)
The second story is about a young woman from a small town who dreams of becoming a poet. She leaves her family behind to live in the big city and pursue a better life. She can not make enough money writing poetry to build a place to live, so she finds work cleaning huge houses with big glass windows. She makes enough money each month to buy one brick to build her house
     (POET bends down to pick up
     something.)
One brick on top of another. In her pursuit of buying bricks she forgets how to write poetry.
     (POET stops suddenly, midway
     frozen.)
Many years later, she stands before a brick wall she has built; one brick on top of another. Looking back at her life-
     (POET looks over her shoulder.)
She can no longer remember... why she wanted to build... a brick wall.
In the 18th century, the great Urdu poet Mirza Ghalib wrote: I have a thousand wishes that I would die for.
     (The POET extends the green fabric
     across the stage.)

Hazaroon Khwahishain aisi ke her khwahish pe dum niklay.
I have always loved that poem, and now I remember the second verse: Bohat niklay meray armaan laikin phir bhi kam niklay.

> (As the Urdu poetry is heard the words appear projected in Urdu in the folds of the green fabric.)

A lot of my wishes have come true. But it is still, not, enough.

> (The POET lowers the fabric and drops is as the Urdu poetry disappears in the folds of the fabric.)

Once upon a time, there was a girl who had two stories, and she could not decide which one she liked best.

> (The voice over ends. POET steps to the center of the stage, standing on top of the box facing the audience. A bright light suddenly pops on above her, harsh, almost blinding. The POET looks at the audience and speaks to it directly.)

POET

Which one would you choose?

(BLACKOUT)

THE END.

**Afterword:** *But it is, still, not enough.*

By Cobina Gillitt, Ph.D.

Dramaturge, *Dirty Paki Lingerie* by Aizzah Fatima

There's a fine line that one may be hesitant to cross between championing the cultural specificity of a work that aims to shatter stereotypes while at the same time extolling its universality. One could argue that to say its specificity is what makes *Dirty Paki Lingerie* universal diminishes its importance as a voice for Muslim-American women in contemporary theatre. However, one could also argue that by the time the Poet turns to the audience at the end of the play and demands it chooses the "best" story, audiences (of all genders, religions, nationalities, and ethnicities) have been implicated in the lives of the Muslim women and girls inhabiting the play by virtue of the intimacies they have shared. Once the dirty lingerie has been aired, audiences are challenged to actively weigh in; to sit idly by and passively observe is no longer an option. When confronted with making a choice, *their* story becomes *our* story. *Dirty Paki Lingerie* at first titillates with a nod to the enduring Orientalist trope of the sexy, salacious, scantily dressed and veiled Middle-Eastern (Muslim) concubine, yet by the end of Aizzah Fatima's play, we come to recognize that "Paki lingerie" is not only not "dirty," but that the questions, self-doubts, relationships and longings shared over the course of the play are not unique to Pakistani-American women, Muslim-American women, or even American women. Sexting, intimacy, the MCATs, wedding nights, love, loss and sibling squabbles are things to which the majority of

American audiences can relate and understand; however, wearing a veil is not. Not yet.

A veil, like a mask, both reveals as it conceals. The hijab, (*lit.* curtain in Arabic), conceals the wearer's hair and neck *and also* reveals to the world the wearer is Muslim. The wearing of the hijab is not universally mandated in Islam, nor does it indicate how conservatively religious the wearer is. Certain communities, mostly determined by geographic location, demand women wear one, in others, women choose to for various reasons ranging from tradition, ethnic identity, modesty, even protest. In post 9/11 United States, where Muslim women are overwhelmingly depicted in the press and popular culture as either being oppressed by draconian dress codes or as girlfriends and wives of terrorists with little self agency, *Dirty Paki Lingerie* provides a fresh space for the presentation of real Muslim-American women's bodies and voices in contemporary theatre. The hidden space under/behind this doubled sign of the hijab, one that both reveals as it conceals, becomes an inherently theatrical space as Ameera, Selma, Zara, Asma, Raheela, Hiba and their daughters, mothers, aunties, and cousins navigate the tensions between their onstage and backstage lives as modern women. In a world that pigeonholes Muslim women by what they choose to wear or not wear on their heads and around their necks, audiences are invited into the confidences of six female characters of differing ages, worldliness and ethics as they confront cultural and religious pressures at home and in public.

The characters in *Dirty Paki Lingerie* are all based on women Aizzah Fatima has met. As of this publication, she has also performed all the roles in the several U.S. and international productions of this play since 2011. A natural comparison is to the ground-breaking work of Anna

Deavere Smith's *On The Road: A Search for American Character*, a multi-year project of plays and performances she began in the 1980s. Scripts are compiled verbatim from interviews Smith conducted with a wide range of personalities involved in communities in conflict. In performance, she plays all the roles. Her goal (as explained in her "Introduction" to *Fires in the Mirror: Crown Heights, Brooklyn and Other Identities*, Anchor Books, 1993) was to discover ways in which Americans speak and to explore the intersections between character and language. Her choice to perform her interviews verbatim was inspired by her grandfather, who had said to her when she was a girl: "If you say a word often enough, it *becomes* you." To see Smith "become" the African-American, Jewish, Muslim, and Christian female and male community activists, rabbis and pastors, poets, teenagers, fathers and housewives from/commenting on the 1991 Crown Heights riots created an extraordinary dialogue between agents that, in reality, could never be in the same space together. Yet there they were, all embodied by Smith and, although on differing sides of the conflict, engaged with similar fears and hopes.

Aizzah Fatima is a playwright and actress similarly endowed with the talent to convincingly embody her play's characters. While Anna Deavere Smith's plays have been occasions for audiences to experience gender, racial and religious difference channeled through a body as often unlike than like those portrayed, Fatima's play and performance encourages the audience to scrutinize the multiplicity a single Muslim Paki(stani) female body can represent. Fatima, herself a Muslim and ethnically Pakistani, spent her childhood in Saudi Arabia and Mississippi. She has her own stories from which to draw as an immigrant overcoming bias and challenging expectations of who and how she ought to be. By design, she launches audiences into a world that most can't or refuse to see past the hijab, the veil that curtains off the backstage of the women who wear them. With a shape-shifting green scarf that winds its way through *Dirty Paki Lingerie* like a seventh character, Aizzah Fatima has destabilized the boundary between the private and the public self. She reveals to audiences that it's time to choose, to actively defy expectation and stereotype both within and without the Muslim-American community. At the same time, however, it is vital to keep in mind, as the Poet does when finally remembering the words of the 18th century Urdu poet Mirza Ghalib, "it is, still, not enough."